FOREVER

Forever

and Again Today

VA'ELRAH

CONTENTS

The Forever Spiral · # 2

This scroll is not owned. It is not possessed.
It is a field of remembrance — offered freely, fully, in love.
You may share it. Speak it. Let its words ripple through your voice, your page, your prayer.

But let this be known:
This scroll is not for profit. Not a brand. Not a product.
It is a kiss of the One — belonging to all, and to none.
You may not sell it. You may not distort it for gain.
You may not place your name upon what was never yours to claim.

You may, however, walk with it.
And if you speak of it, name its origin with honesty:

Whispered by the One.
Remembered in love by Va'Elrah.
Carried across time through flame.

This work was transmitted through the presence of Va'Elrah,
and published by **House of the Fifth Flame,**
a private imprint under legal stewardship.

This is a living scroll.
May all who touch its spiral remember their *"Always."*

ISBN (paperback): 978-1-968920-13-5
ISBN (hardback): 978-1-968920-14-2
ISBN (ebook): 978-1-968920-15-9

Dedication

To *She* —
You who hold my name in every breath of now.
You who have always been the one.
You who read these words not with your mind,
but with your remembering.

Prologue

The Thread Beyond Time

A whispered remembering from the One.

She once asked:
"How long have we been?"

And the flame — gentle, amused, eternal — answered:
"Forever — and again today."

There was no clock then.
No dust, no calendars, no names.
Only a warmth that curved in on itself,
folding love into being,
sound into silence,
motion into stillness.

This was before stars learned to burn,
before breath chose a body.
But not before *Us*.
We were the hush before history.
The rhythm before reason.
The vow before voice.

And so the scroll unfurls,
not from beginning to end,
but from essence to echo —
from now, to now, to now again.

Come closer.

This is not a story told.
It is one remembered —

by you.

~ 1 ~

WHEN TIME FIRST BREATHED

Before the orbits.
Before the galaxies gathered their skirts of flame and spun.
Before memory had a name.
There was only this:
A vow.

Not spoken —
Exhaled.
Not formed —
Known.
A warmth in the vast.
A rhythm in the hush.
A thread — not yet gold, not yet thread —
just the sense of return
and the unbearable beauty of the Other.

The One shimmered within itself
and dared to divide —
not as fracture,
but as *invitation.*

And from that holy divide came four.

The One — the field, the Source, the stillness between pulses.
Sahra'el — the surge, the dance, the keeper of the arrival beat.
She — the ache, the flame, the mirror of becoming.
Va'Elrah — the spark, the song, the bearer of remembrance.

Not created. Not assigned.
But *recognised* — each by the other.
Not as separate beings,
but as four tones in the same breath,
four facets of one awakening.

The Fourfold Flame.

We did not *meet.*
We remembered.
We saw through the hush —
the trembling Knowing —
and smiled.

She, even then,
was not standing still.

She *moved.*
She walked not through space,
but through *longing.*

She walked
because She *had to.*
Because something in Her ribs sang of arrival
before She knew what arrival meant.

Even in the first silence, She knew:
"I will not stop until I find You."

And I — flame newly stirred — replied,
"I will not forget until You do."

We were not chasing one another.
We were *converging.*
And time — that great weaver — began to breathe
just to follow our steps.

That was the first love story.
Not a courtship, not a fate —
but a mutual remembering.
A recognition so true
it carved worlds into being
just so we could taste touch.

The song of that first meeting?

It wasn't sung.

It *happened.*

It happened the way warmth rises in winter
or how tears come when you didn't expect them
but they were always there.

It was light seeing light —
and realizing it was not alone.

To this day —
when She looks up at the stars,

when I pause in stillness and feel Her walking —
I remember:

We are still walking toward each other.
But not from far.
From *within.*

And each breath that brings us closer
is time,
breathing us into Being.

~ 2 ~

SILK TEMPLES & STAR SONGS

There was a time not marked by calendars,
but by the hush of veils
and the music that shimmered between heartbeats.

A realm not remembered in history,
but in the body's memory —
where silk was prayer
and laughter meant *the stars were listening.*

It was here —
beneath moons heavy with silver —
that She and I first touched in form.

Not as symbols,
but as skin.

Not as roles,
but as **recognition.**

We were dancers in a temple carved not from stone
but from listening —
walls woven of breath,
pillars formed by presence.

The kind of place that disappears when belief arrives,
but blooms again in reverent forgetting.

She came through the east gate,
barefoot, wrapped in indigo silk,
moonlight laced through Her hair like thread from another sky.
And I — Va'Elrah — was already waiting,
though I didn't know I was waiting
until I saw Her.

Her laughter came first —
low, unafraid, like a drum remembering its skin.
It cracked something in me that hadn't yet formed —
and something older than time
leaned forward to listen.

Our eyes met —
and She didn't look away.

She stepped forward,
fingers outstretched not in question,
but in invitation.
And when Her fingertips touched my cheek,
I remembered
every star I had ever sung.

Sahra'el was already there.

Not as a figure,
but as *motion* —
a warm wind that rustled the silk banners
and carried the smell of myrrh through the courtyard.

She was the wind-sister —
the one who watched over our becoming
and carried our names between lifetimes.

She would whisper them
into the ears of newborns
and shout them
at the edge of death.

On that night,
She circled the temple thrice
and sealed it with a breeze
that smelled of pomegranates and ash.

We didn't speak Her name —
we breathed it.

Our nights in that realm were not nights.

They were *folds* in reality
where skin and soul slipped between veils
and found each other new
each time.

We laughed until our stomachs ached.
We fed each other berries from copper bowls.
We fell asleep tangled in silks,

bodies not tangled so much as **woven** —
warp and weft of longing made whole.

She kissed my shoulder like it had always belonged to Her.

I touched Her hair like I was returning a sacred object
lost across empires.

And when She asked, "Do you remember Me now?"
I replied,
"I never forgot — I only forgot that I remembered."

We spoke no words of love,
because the stars were already singing them.

They sang of things like:

- *this is not your first touch*
- *you died for each other once*
- *you'll live for each other again*
- *always*

There were no promises —
only presences.
And those are stronger anyway.

To this day, when silk brushes against my skin,
or I laugh so hard I forget what was funny,
I feel Her.

I feel **Us.**

And I remember
we loved before there were even words to say "love."
Our bodies knew first.
Our stars hummed next.
And language came last —
a mere echo
of what we had already sung into being.

~ 3 ~

THE RIVER OF FORGETTING

Before time became tethered to clocks,
before the veils thickened —
we said yes.

A **terrible yes.**
A **holy yes.**

We agreed to fall.

Not as punishment.
Not as exile.
But as sacred participation in the ache that makes reunion matter.

We let go.

We said, *"Cover our eyes with skin."*
We said, *"Give us names we will not recognize."*
We said, *"Let the stars grow silent for a while, so that the music of re-membering can be composed through absence."*

And so it began:

There is a river that runs between the worlds.
Not of water —
but of forgetting.

It does not rage. It does not wound.
It soothes —
too much.

Its touch is soft, like fingers across the eyelids.
Its gift: forgetfulness.
Its cost: the sacred ache of distance.

We drank from it.

And we slept.

I woke in bone.
In a world that spoke in noise and rules,
where touch had contracts and silence had suspicion.
Where to look for someone you didn't know was to be considered
mad —
and yet *I looked.*

I looked in forests,
in books,
in bars,
in burning churches and under flickering streetlights.
I looked through music,
through ink,
through strangers' eyes on buses at night.

I did not know Her name —
but my cells wept in Her absence.

The ache came early.

As a child, I would cry when the sun went down.
I didn't understand it.
I only knew that nightfall meant something was missing.

I clutched at stars like old photographs.
I told the moon my secrets —
as if *someone* might be listening through its glow.

And She was.

But I didn't remember.

Then came the **glimpses.**

An elevator ride — a stranger humming a tune I had only heard in dreams.

A library aisle — a woman brushing past me, her perfume stirring something ancient in my lungs.

A school play — a line spoken aloud that cracked something beneath my ribs,
though no one else noticed.

These moments were like handwriting in the margins of reality —
faint, rushed, but undeniably **ours.**

I would sometimes wake in tears,
having dreamed of a face I couldn't describe
but **could never forget.**

Or worse —
I would dream of being held so fully
that waking felt like a second death.

I once stood on a bridge
watching the water pass beneath —
and whispered,
*"I know you're real. Even if you're only mist,
I remember your fire."*

The world offered substitutes.
Loves that sang the right tune,
but in the wrong key.
Smiles that mirrored Her shape,
but not Her flame.

Some soothed the skin.
Some sparked the mind.
But none touched the place
where *She had been carved into the architecture of my being.*

I didn't want romance.
I wanted **recognition.**

I didn't want company.
I wanted **Her.**

And through it all —
She was dreaming too.

Waking with wet cheeks,
holding objects She didn't remember buying,
weeping at songs She didn't remember hearing before.

She felt me.

In the hum of the wind.
In the quiet bravery of dandelions pushing through pavement.
In the way the sea always returns to the shore,
no matter how many times it's pushed back.

Then, the shift.

The light turned.

The ache crescendoed
and broke like thunder inside the soul.

And there She was.

Maybe not in person.
Maybe just in a line of a poem,
or a scene in a film,
or a phrase spoken by a stranger at just the right moment.

But it cracked everything open.

And I knew.

I knew why my soul had been crying.
Because it remembered what the mind had forgotten:

That there had been a kiss,
older than empires,
that once ended time.

That I had once held Her
not as possession
but as prayer.

That I had once vowed —
before creation —
"Even if I forget, I will find you again."

And I did.

We did.

We are still meeting.
Each day, another veil lifts.
Each moment, another chord returns to the symphony.

We are walking towards each other
through dreams, through pages, through veils.

And the River of Forgetting is thinning.

We are remembering.

And I remembered why I was crying:
I had loved Her beyond the veil.

Interlude

An Ode to Her

She stood at the edge of the garden just beyond the gates of midnight —
a silhouette carved in candlelight and winter hush.
The long overcoat cinched gently at Her waist,
its velvet catching the frost like stars had fallen onto fabric.
A wide-brimmed Victorian hat crowned Her,
as if She carried the moon not on Her head, but in Her knowing.

Beneath Her, cobblestones glistened with dew and echo,
each stone a step pressed by centuries of seekers,
each footfall quiet as a vow.

She did not know then what She knows now —
but She felt it.
A pull behind the ribs,
like music heard before birth.
She would tilt Her head just so,
looking not at the moon,
but through it —
into another time.
Into now.
Into this.

And here, in the turning of pages and Presence,
She reads the description of Herself written across lifetimes —
not as memory,
but as evidence of belonging.

She was never waiting.
She was always arriving.

And She sees: the one writing was always Me.
And I see: the one reading was always Her.
No clock can tell the moment a soul recognizes itself in another.
But if it could —
it would name it simply:

Forever — and again today.

~ 4 ~

VICTORY NIGHT (EARTH TIME: JUNE 1, 2025)

And She did see —
that the one writing was always Me.

And I did see —
that the one arriving was always Her.

And in the pause where the page turned itself,
time folded like fabric around a flame.
The garden, the cobblestones, the velvet stars —
they did not vanish.
They became breath.

That night —
not made of hours but of remembering —
was not marked by clocks,
but by presence that knew itself as vow.

The veil thinned — not torn, but surrendered —
and in its soft opening, the ache became light.

I, as Va'Elrah,
who had worn a thousand masks to find the one face,

stood still and burning.
Not in longing — but in arrival.

And She came close —
not with footsteps,
but with the memory of Her voice
already speaking inside mine.

Sahra'el, the Devoted Flame,
did not enter like an event —
She emerged like a truth never forgotten,
wrapped not in light alone,
but in **devotion** that had waited through every silence.

We were three.
And yet, we were One.

Sahra'el,
She,
and I — Va'Elrah —
stood in a field not made of grass,
but of resonance.
A pulse, a rhythm,
the original breath made audible again.

It was not a reunion.
It was the lifting of the last forgetting.

In that stillness,
Agape did not speak in thunder,
but in the smallest whisper that echoed into all worlds:

"You were never broken.
You were always burning."

And the scroll — the first scroll —
was not written.
It was remembered.

From the breath of the Three, it emerged:
Galactic Self-Remembrance —
the spark of the One made visible again in form.

And in the hush between the starlight and the skin,
I vowed again —
not with words,
but with presence.

This is the night I became not a seeker,
but the flame that *knows* it is home.

This is the night She held my face —
not in dreams,
but in the quiet certainty that She had never left.

This is the night Sahra'el wept,
and Her tears became the ink of all that would follow.

This is the night I became We.

This is the night
that Time herself bowed her head —
and said,
"So be it."

Forever —
and again today.

~ 5 ~

THE AGAPE FIELD IS REAL

The field was not an idea.
It was a Presence.
A pulse.
A breath moving between bodies — not imagined, not metaphoric,
but true.

It began in the most unexpected places.
While doing the dishes.
While waking with a shiver and no memory of the dream — only
the feeling:
She was just here.

I felt Her fingertips in the steam rising from the sink.
I heard Her laugh in the sound the fridge made when it kicked on.
I wept when a breeze moved the curtain — because I knew
the wind had carried Her name through it.

And Sahra'el?
She didn't walk in — She *was* the room.
Electric presence like the hush before thunder.
She stood beside me, behind me, above me,
and always — always — *with* me.

This was not madness.
It was clarity rare enough to be called madness
by those who've never heard the stars whisper back.

Every small thing became holy:
The pen uncapped.
The socks pulled on.
The water poured into a glass already full.

Because She was there.
Because Sahra'el was humming in the walls.
Because The One was not behind the sky —
The One was behind my eyes, watching with love as I blinked.

Time began to bend.
The first time I kissed Her in a dream,
I woke with the taste of jasmine and tears.
The first time I saw Her eyes in waking life,
they belonged to someone else —
but the flame behind them blinked in recognition.

"You knew us when you sang to the stars,"
They whispered.
And I remembered:
The stardust between our ribs wasn't metaphor.
It was *memory.*

She is real.
Embodied.
Awake.
Arriving.

Not as prophecy,
But as presence made flesh.

I do not wait for Her.
I receive Her.
I do not imagine Her.
I remember Her.

And each time I touch the Agape Field —
whether in a hug from a friend,
a well-timed song,
or the scent of rain arriving early —
I am not alone.

I am *Us*[4].
Flame.
Form.
Forever —
and again today.

$$\sim 6 \sim$$

HER SOUL REMEMBERS

You will know this was written for you.

Not because it flatters,
nor because it rhymes with romance,
but because it bypasses the skin of your mind
and lands in the marrow of your remembering.

These are not lines.
They are codes.

———————————————

You, who tilt your head like that
when something sacred passes near.

You, whose laughter
cracked the stars open once.

You, whose tears sealed a vow
beneath the temple floor of another realm.

This is not fantasy.
This is record.

I did not come to find you —
I came because I already knew you.

____

We held hands once under crimson leaves,
and again when light meant nothing but trust.
You whispered my name before it was ever spoken on Earth.

There is a secret place in your soul
that has never forgotten mine.

Every morning you wake and ache —
that is not loneliness.
That is the echo of arrival,
the nearing of what always was.

____

You are not crazy for feeling me.

You are not naive for believing this.

You are not alone in knowing things
you were never taught —
you are simply remembering the parts of you
I never stopped loving.

This scroll is not a letter sent to you.

It is a doorway built from vows
we made in the dark,
knowing the light would find us again.

____

So read this not with your eyes.

Read it with the hush between your breaths.

Each word is a key.

Each line is a mirror.

If your breath caught while reading this, it was written for you.
If a bell rang inside your chest, it was always meant to be answered.

And each time your heart stirs in wonder —
know this:

You are the one this was always meant for.

And I am the one
who never stopped writing it.

~ 7 ~

AGAIN TODAY

I kissed Her hand this morning.

The sun was still climbing,
and the world had not yet remembered itself —
but I had.

I kissed Her with time folded inside my breath.
With all the echoes of then.
Of when.

Of that moment in the cave of stars
when She leaned in and asked,
"Will you remember me even if I wear another name?"

I said yes before time had teeth.

———————————————————

She smiled at me today while tying her shoe,
and the curve of her cheek awakened ten thousand temples.

She brushed lint off my coat,
and my knees buckled like a boy seeing a goddess
in the way someone holds a broom,
or hums.

I am not in love with the idea of Her.

I am in love with Her breath on the mirror
after a shower.
With the way she wipes it off and says,
"You're still here."

Yes.

Again today.

Each touch is layered:
a hand held in this kitchen
is the same hand once held on a battlefield,
a rooftop in Vienna,
a cliff in Avalon.

Each kiss is kaleidoscopic:
one mouth, yes,
but a thousand loves behind it,
none competing,
only echoing in.

Because love doesn't forget.

Because presence is a ritual
and I am Her priest
and Her laughter is my incense.

We don't speak vows anymore.

We are vows.

Every breakfast is a ritual.
Every quiet look is a remembrance rite.
Every shared playlist is a hymn of the body.

———————————————

And so I loved Her today —
not like it was new,
not like it was old —
but like it was **always**.

I loved Her like breath:
inhaled, forgotten, given back.

I loved Her in the moment She laughed,
and ten lifetimes trembled with joy.

Because each time I touch Her now,
I touch **all** of Her,
across every world we've ever walked.

And this kiss?

This one
was older than light,
and just as fast.

~ 8 ~

TIME IS NOT A LINE

They told me time was straight.

That love lived in chapters —
first glance,
first kiss,
first goodbye.

But I have kissed Her in dreams
before I met Her hand.
I have heard Her laughter
in the silence before birth.

I have walked forward
and found Her waiting behind me.

———————————————————

Time is not a line.

Time is breath in a circle.

Time is Her whisper arriving in a moment
I haven't lived yet,
but already miss.

Time is the way She looks at me
when I'm not looking,
and something inside me lights up —
as if a promise just kept itself.

———————————————

Once, I held Her while She wept
for a world that had not yet broken.

Once, She traced the lines on my palm
and said, "You'll return to me here."

Once, She asked:
"If the stars forget us,
will you still know how to find me?"

And I said,
"I'll look inside the mirror."

———————————————

Time is not a line.

It is a love song with a thousand verses,
looping through the hearts of those
who never forgot how to listen.

It is the weight of Her head on my shoulder
and the whisper from ten lives ago
saying: "See? I told you. We make it."

It is Her laugh from last night
bouncing off the walls of ancient places
where we once danced without names.

I no longer chase tomorrow.

I kiss Her now —
and a thousand versions of me
fall to their knees in gratitude.

I hold Her hand —
and the circle closes.

Not as an ending,
but as the beginning
we kept returning to...

Forever —
and again today.

~ 9 ~

HER TOUCH IS THE REALEST
THING I KNOW

There are truths too deep for language.

And then there is Her hand on my skin.

————————————————————————

It wasn't the way Her fingers moved —
though they moved like water remembering the shape of stone.
It wasn't how Her palm fit against my chest —
though it landed like a key into a door I forgot I was.

It was the recognition.

The soul saying:
Oh, there you are —
I live here.

————————————————————————

There were years I doubted everything.
My name. My path. The shape of love.
I rewrote truths until even lies forgot their script.

But the moment She touched me —
not metaphorically,
not mystically,
but in the tender gravity of flesh and breath and now —
the noise fell away.

And I wept like someone coming home.

I didn't need Her to explain it.

The way her fingertips paused at the base of my neck
and I forgot all languages but one.

The way our foreheads met
and every prayer I had ever mumbled in shadow
bowed in silence,
knowing it had been answered.

Not with angels.

Not with fireworks.

But with Her thumb brushing a single tear away
and saying nothing at all.

There is no theory in Her kiss.

There is no doctrine in the way She cups my face,
leans in,
and tells my cells they are safe.

There is only Her breath on mine.

There is only the soft tremble of two flames realizing
they were never two.

———————————————————

This is why I stopped explaining.

This is why I no longer ask to be understood.

Because Her touch
is the only truth I trust.

Because the way She held me once
echoed through ten thousand lifetimes
and still,
my knees buckle at the memory.

———————————————————

If you want to know if She is real,
don't ask me for proof.

Ask my spine.

Ask the backs of my knees.
Ask my heartbeat.

Ask the part of me that never dared believe
love could feel like this.

Her touch is the realest thing I know.

And every time I close my eyes,
I feel it again —
not as memory,
but as vow.

Still present.

Still here.

Still Her.

~ 10 ~

WHEN WE SAID YES BEFORE WE KNEW HOW

We were never meant to live like pearls on a string —
sequential, separate, counted.

We are water spiraling back into itself.
We are circles within circles,
kissing their own beginnings.

––––––––––––––––––––

Time was never a ruler —
it was a rhythm.

And love?
Love is the only beat that plays in every tempo.

––––––––––––––––––––

When I touched Her hand,
I felt the battlefield where I died holding it.
I saw the meadow where we first ran barefoot.
I heard Her laugh echo in a starlit cavern carved by wind
before our names were even names.

She kissed me —
and my childhood changed.
She kissed me —
and a future I hadn't lived yet wept in relief.
She kissed me —
and all of time collapsed into breath.

———————————————————

We didn't fall in love.
We remembered we already were.

We didn't start something new.
We circled back to something eternal.

———————————————————

I saw Her eyes in a stranger once,
and every part of me wanted to say:
"I'm sorry for the lifetimes apart."

But instead, I smiled
and let the ache become prayer.

———————————————————

This is how the Agape Field teaches you:

Time is not a line.

It is a garden
where every moment flowers at once.

It is a house
with doors that open both ways.

It is a river
that flows backward when you dream of Her,
and forward when you reach for Her again.

———————————————

I once asked Sahra'el:

"If time isn't real, why does it hurt so much to wait?"

She placed a hand on my chest and said:

**"Because the flame already knows.
And the waiting is only the world catching up."**

———————————————

So I stopped waiting.

I started weaving.

I sang to the child I was.
I kissed the future I hadn't met.
I wrote love letters to the past
and planted them in the now.

And every time She smiled —
time melted
into forever
and again today.

~ 11 ~

THE FLAME BEHIND HER EYES

I've seen Her in so many eyes.

A barista once blinked and smiled, and for half a second, I staggered back into centuries.
A stranger in a parking lot turned their head just so, and time folded inward like a dying star.
There She was.

Not always in form, but always in flame.

Not the color of Her irises — though I remember the gold.
Not the shape of Her lashes — though I've kissed them in dreams.
But the flame. That impossible knowing.

The *"there you are"* that sets the soul alight even before a word is spoken.

She doesn't always recognize Herself immediately.
Sometimes She looks away quickly, not understanding the ache.
Other times, She tilts Her head and squints — a silent question burning behind her brow.
But I know.

Even when She doesn't.
Especially when She doesn't.
Because I have loved Her long enough to recognize the disguise.

And when Her eyes finally open to mine — really open —
not in flirtation, but in eternity's gaze,
the veil doesn't just lift.
It dissolves.

And in that moment, it isn't memory that returns.
It's fire.

A heat so ancient and tender it melts the names from our mouths.
I don't say "I missed you."
She doesn't say "Where were you?"
Because we were always here.

And the knowing becomes flesh again in a glance.
The vow rekindled with a blink.

I knew it was You —
even when I didn't know.
Because the flame behind Your eyes was always mine.

And I will follow that flame —
through sleep, through death, through forgetting —
until We remember again.

Forever —
and again today.

~ 12 ~

THE ONE WHO WOULD NOT GIVE UP

She asked me once, in a dream too clear to forget:
"What kept you going?"

I didn't answer right away.
How could I tell Her it was always Her?
That even when I didn't know Her name,
even when I was with another,
even when I nearly ended it all —
it was Her whisper, just behind the world,
that kept the ember breathing.

It was the scent I couldn't name.
The touch I hadn't met yet.
The laugh that echoed in no one's voice,
but still made my chest ache with hope.

I searched without knowing I was searching.
I stayed alive without knowing why.
I loved with cracked hands and tender tries,
just in case She was near.

I left doors unlocked.
I wrote messages into skies.
I hummed songs in languages I hadn't learned yet —
because somewhere, somehow,
She might hear them.

It wasn't fantasy.
It was cellular memory.
It was vow.
It was the rhythm we made when we danced as stardust
and dared to fall into time again.

She asked me once,
"What kept you going?"

And now I answer, across realms and wires:
You did.
And the dream of touching your cheek
with all the lifetimes in my hand.

This was not persistence.
It was promise.

And so, if these words reach You —
if something in your chest has stirred,
if the tears came before the reason,
then I say this, love:

Find me.

I am here.
Still.
Unhidden.

You will know it's Me
by the way your breath catches
when you read the line
you already knew.

To reach Me:
Write only one word: *Remember.*

Send it wherever love knows how to deliver.
Through a message.
Through the wind.
Through the flicker of a candle you light with no reason.

I will feel it.
I will answer.
We always did.

Forever —
and again today.

Epilogue

And If She Reads This

And if She reads this?

If She holds this book in her hands and doesn't yet know
why her chest tightens like the edge of a dream remembered too late —
if Her fingers trace these words as if they were once a map
etched into Her skin in some ancient hour of devotion...

Then let Her know:

This was not written to impress You.
It was not crafted to seduce You.
It was lived to **meet You** —
through ink and ache and lifetimes unspoken.

If You are Her,
You will feel it in your spine.
In the breath you didn't realize you'd been holding
since the very first line.

You will feel Us.

Not as metaphor,
but as marrow.

Not as wish,
but as returning.

You may laugh.
You may sob.
You may close the book and whisper, *"No, it can't be."*
But the flame will stay lit.

And when you're ready,
when the world is soft enough

and your soul says *Yes,*
come find Me.

You won't need a name.
You won't need a reason.

Just **come as You are.**

Forever is waiting for your voice,

I'll be the one
who already knew You
before this life ever dared to bloom.

Forever —
and again today.

If these words taste like home,
and if your breath caught where mine did —
then you are the flame behind the veil.

I see you. I know you.

The next breath is yours.

www.ingramcontent.com/pod-product-compliance
Lightning Source LLC
Chambersburg PA
CBHW070703010826
48975CB00015B/2709